In memory of my great-great-grandfather Victor Jones Sr.,
who was twenty years old at the time of the first Juneteenth
and died a free man in 1928 —G.A.

This book is dedicated to my daughter, Nora,
for being the light in my life and for insisting that
I try various creative outlets and forms of expression.
And to all my strong, resilient, and amazing ancestors,
who paved the way for me to be here today. —C.B.

Visit us on the Web! rhcbooks.com

Educators and librarians, for a variety of teaching tools,
visit us at RHTeachersLibrarians.com

Library of Congress Cataloging-in-Publication Data
Names: Armand, Glenda, author. | Barksdale, Corey (Illustrator), illustrator.
Title: The night before freedom: a Juneteenth story / words by Glenda Armand; pictures by Corey Barksdale.
Description: First edition. | New York: Crown Books for Young Readers, [2023]
Audience: Ages 4–8. | Audience: Grades K–1. | Summary: Eight-year-old David and his family gather
at Grandma's house in Galveston, Texas, for a cherished family tradition—Grandma's annual retelling of the story
of Juneteenth, the holiday that commemorates the end of slavery in the United States.
Identifiers: LCCN 2022035953 | ISBN 978-0-593-56746-3 (trade)
ISBN 978-0-593-64533-8 (lib. bdg.) | ISBN 978-0-593-56747-0 (ebook)
Subjects: CYAC: Juneteenth—Fiction. | African Americans—Fiction. | Family life—Fiction.
Texas—History—1865–1950—Fiction. | Picture books.
Classification: LCC PZ7.A697 Ni 2023 | DDC [E]—dc23

The artist used mixed media, including acrylic, oil, and pastel
watercolor pencils on Masonite, to create the illustrations for this book.
The text of this book is set in 18-point Legacy Square ITC and 17-point Plantin Head.
Design by Brittany Ramirez

MANUFACTURED IN CHINA
10 9 8 7 6 5 4 3 2 1
First Edition

THE NIGHT BEFORE
FREEDOM

A JUNETEENTH STORY

WORDS BY GLENDA ARMAND
PICTURES BY COREY BARKSDALE

Crown Books for Young Readers ♛ New York

"Is Grandma going to tell the story?" I asked Dad as the last float in the parade passed by.

"She sure is, David," said Dad. "It wouldn't be Juneteenth if she didn't."

"I can't wait!" I said.

We had come to celebrate Juneteenth with our relatives in Galveston, Texas. All day there had been parades and speeches and lots of food and music. It was a time to remember June 19, 1865, the day when the news of the Emancipation Proclamation arrived in Galveston.

Now my family was gathered at Grandma's house. Aunts, uncles, and cousins were waiting for her to tell the story of the first Juneteenth, when *her* grandmother Mom Bess was only six years old. Grandma still remembered the story just the way Mom Bess used to tell it.

At last, Grandma eased into her rocking chair. It was time!
We kids rushed over and sat on the floor around her. Everyone,
young and old, hushed as Grandma got a faraway look in her
eyes and began.

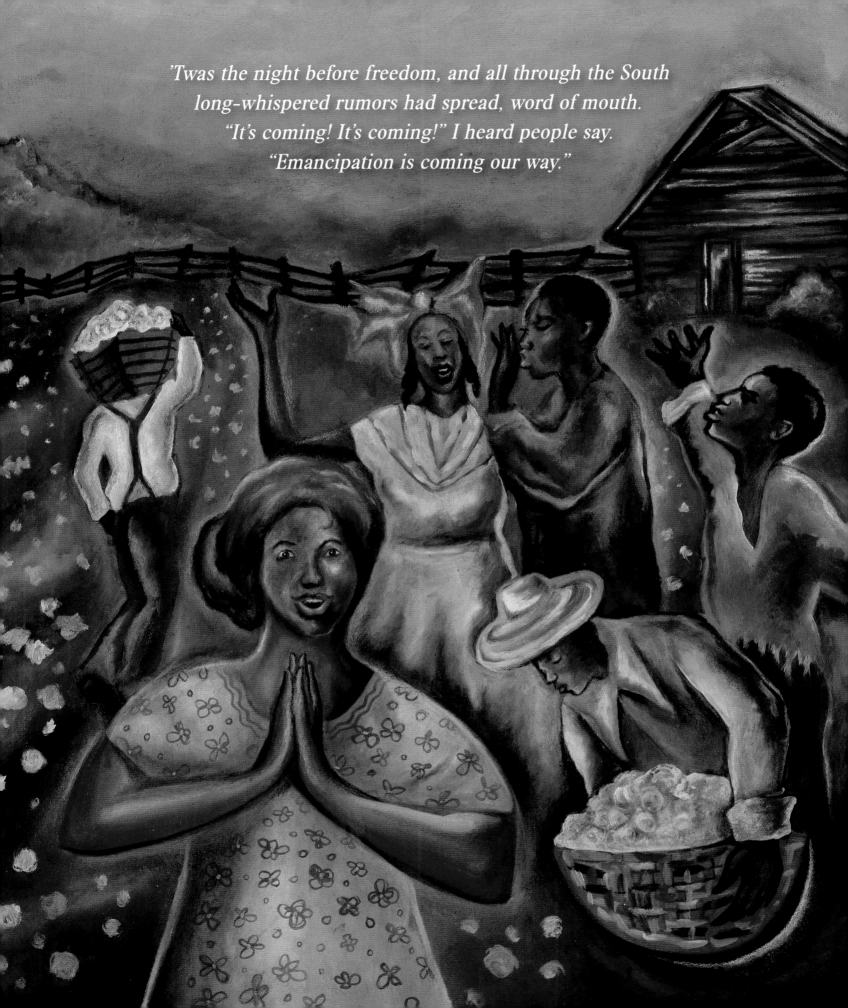

'Twas the night before freedom, and all through the South
long-whispered rumors had spread, word of mouth.
"It's coming! It's coming!" I heard people say.
"Emancipation is coming our way."

Freedom was something that I'd never seen.
What would it look like, and what would it mean?

*A rainbow, said some, would appear sea to sea,
and then we'd sprout wings and we'd fly away free.*

While Mama and Papa slept soundly in bed,
visions of liberty danced in my head.
The very next day was the nineteenth of June;
freedom arrived at the stroke of high noon.

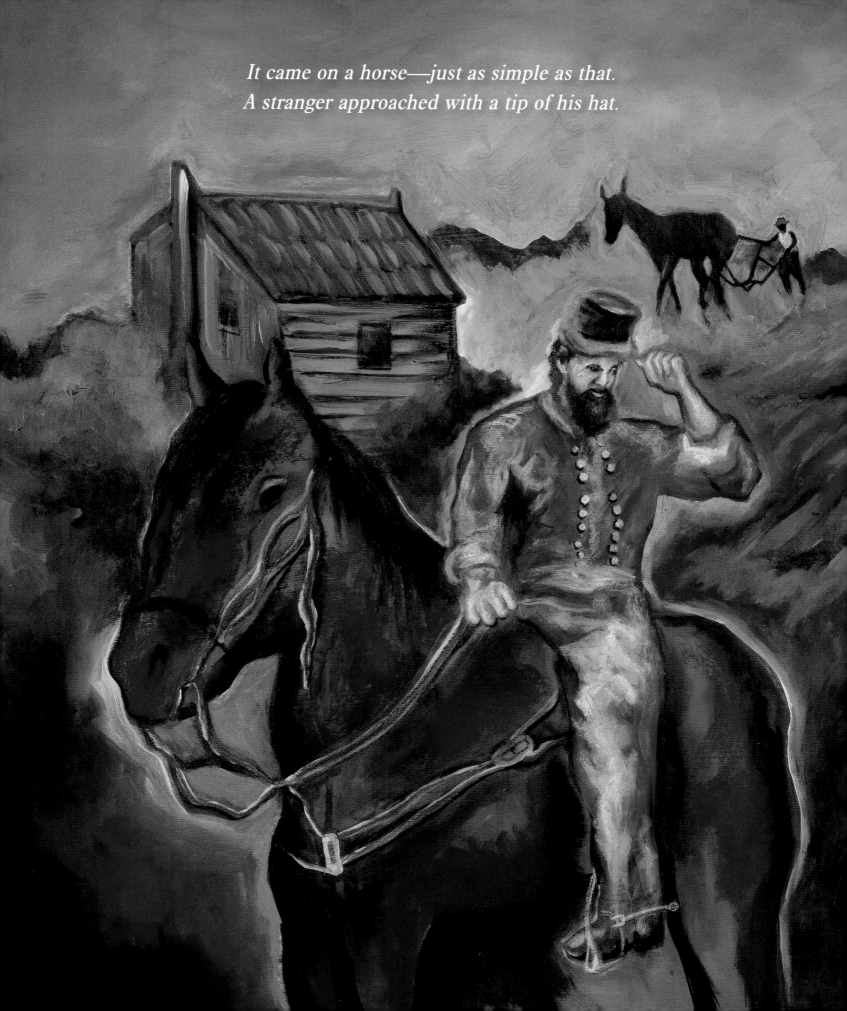

It came on a horse—just as simple as that.
A stranger approached with a tip of his hat.

"Hear ye!" he cried, and we knew right away;
somehow, we knew that today was the day.

He held up a scroll as we gathered around;
some left behind tools they had dropped on the ground.
At first, I stood still as the man slowly read;
then I trembled with joy at each word that he said:

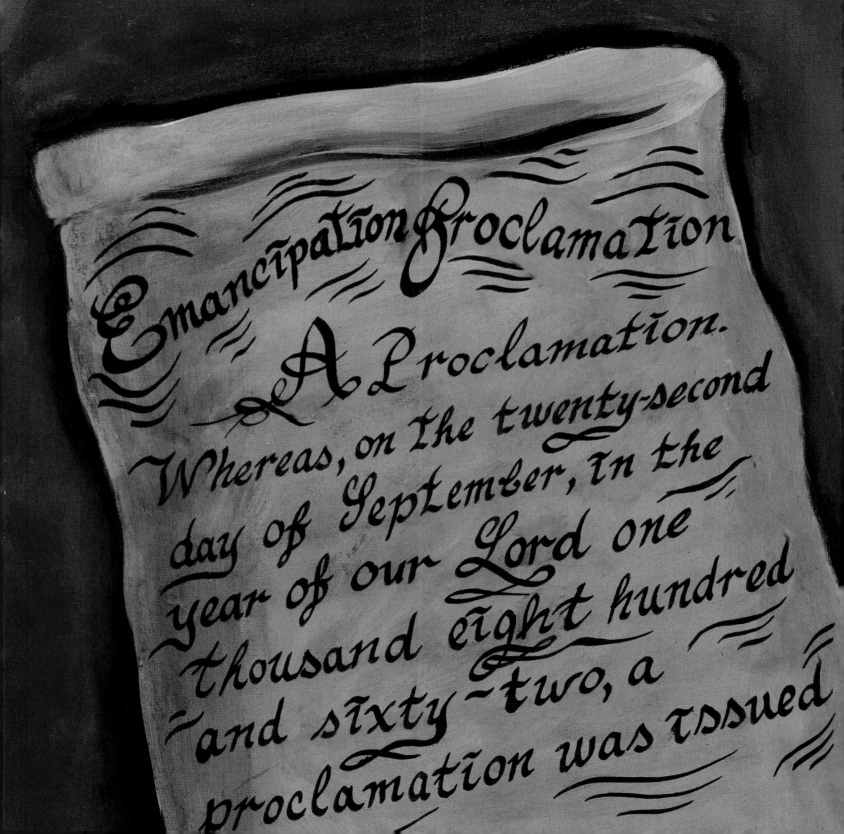

"People of Texas, by this proclamation,
you are hereby informed of your emancipation.
This involves absolute equality.
You are now, henceforward, and forever free."

Emancipation Proclamation

A Proclamation.

Whereas, on the twenty-second day of September, In the year of our Lord one thousand eight hundred and sixty-two, a proclamation was issued

As the man on the horse read the words on the scroll,
a burden seemed lifted from each tired soul.
I heard singing and shouting and cries of "We're free!"
There was hugging and dancing—a true sight to see.

Papa swept Mama right off her feet,
then spun me around as my heart skipped a beat!
But no rainbows appeared; no one took to the sky.
I could not understand, so I asked Mama why.

"Bess," Mama said, smiling, "we're not taking flight;
freedom means claiming our God-given right
to work for ourselves and to learn and to play,
to own our own land and to have our own say."

The words that she spoke were so simple and clear;
I now understood what made freedom so dear.
I wouldn't trade all of those wonderful things
for a bright-colored rainbow or gossamer wings!

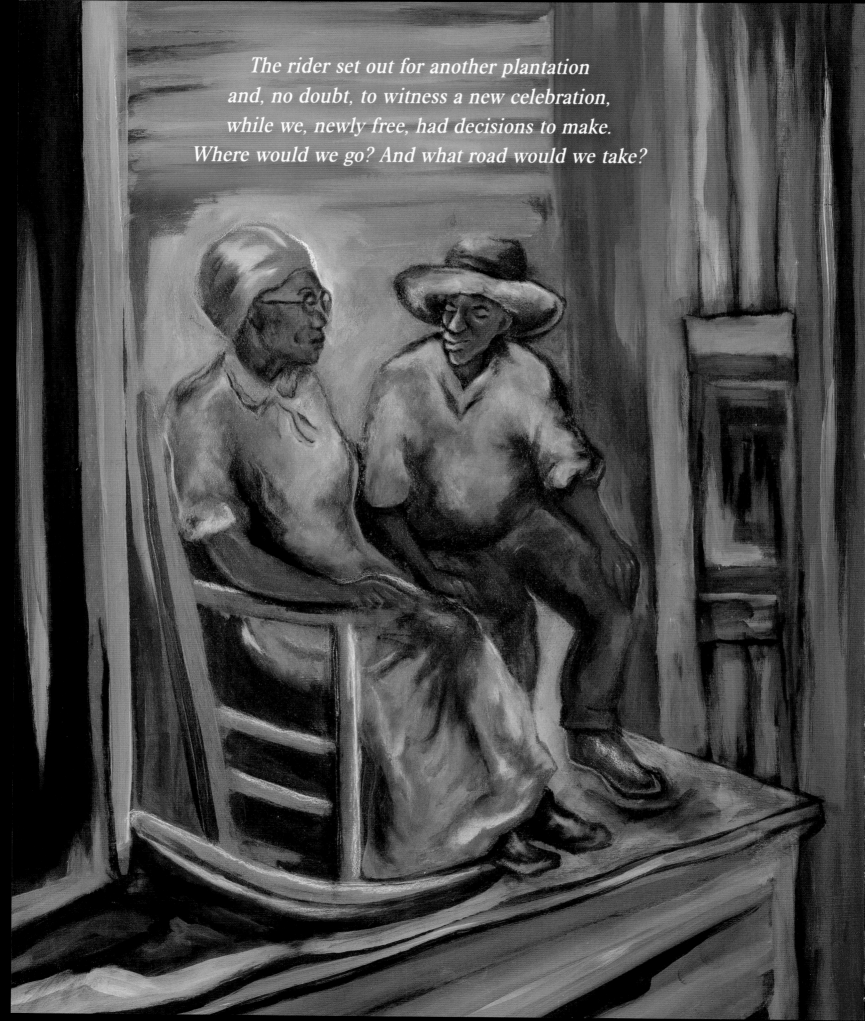

The rider set out for another plantation
and, no doubt, to witness a new celebration,
while we, newly free, had decisions to make.
Where would we go? And what road would we take?

Mama and Papa planned all through the night.
I knew, from their words, that our future looked bright.
They were happy and hopeful and serious, too.
So I fell asleep knowing my dream had come true.

Papa kept plowing the red Texas clay.
He worked hard as ever but now received pay.
We bought our own land, and our family grew.
In good times and bad times, our love saw us through.

We enjoyed all the things that true liberty brings.
I learned reading and writing, and that gave me wings!
And as I look back, I am still filled with awe
and still dream of the things that I heard and I saw.

I see all the dancing and hugging and tears;
but now, in my mind's eye, a rainbow appears.
And spanning the rainbow are words all can see:
We are now, henceforward, and forever free.

AFTERWORD

On September 22, 1862, in the midst of the Civil War, President Abraham Lincoln signed a preliminary Emancipation Proclamation. It declared that if the Southern states did not cease their rebellion by January 1, 1863, all enslaved persons within the rebellious states would "be then, thenceforward, and forever free." When the Southern states continued their rebellion, President Lincoln issued the Emancipation Proclamation, effective New Year's Day, 1863.

However, people in Texas did not receive the news of their emancipation until two and a half years later. On June 19, 1865, Major General Gordon Granger arrived in Galveston, Texas, and read General Order No. 3: "The people of Texas are informed that, in accordance with a proclamation from the Executive of the United States, all slaves are free. This involves an absolute equality of personal rights and rights of property between former masters and slaves, and the connection heretofore existing between them becomes that between employer and hired labor."

Six months later, all enslaved persons in the United States were emancipated with the adoption of the Thirteenth Amendment to the United States Constitution on December 6, 1865. Nevertheless, June 19, 1865, the date the news of freedom arrived in Texas, has been celebrated for years in many states to commemorate the end of slavery. In 1979, Juneteenth (June 19) became a state holiday in Texas. On June 17, 2021, President Joe Biden signed a law making Juneteenth a federal holiday.

The Night Before Freedom is also a tribute to *The Night Before Christmas* by Clement C. Moore. In addition to having borrowed some words and images, I wrote *The Night Before Freedom* in the same meter as the classic poem: anapestic tetrameter. That is a mouthful! It simply means that the pattern, or meter, of the poem goes like this: da da DUM da da DUM da da DUM da da DUM. For young Bess, I think that looking forward to freedom was much like the anticipation many children feel when they are waiting for a special day like Christmas.